Christmas at

Henderson's Ranch

a Night Stalkers romance story
by
M. L. Buchman

Buchman Bookworks

Other works by M.L. Buchman

Where Dreams Reside
Maria's Christmas Table
Where Dreams Unfold
Where Dreams Are Written

<u>Dieties Anonymous</u>
Cookbook from Hell: Reheated
Saviors 101

<u>Thrillers</u>
Swap Out!
One Chef!
Two Chef!

<u>SF/F Titles</u>
Nara
Monk's Maze

1

"This isn't right!"

Chelsea Bridges leaned forward to see
what Emily Beale was looking at. Chelsea
didn't see a thing wrong, but then she'd
never been to central Montana before. Out
the small plane's front windshield were
miles and miles of rolling green prairie.
Streams crisscrossed the grassland in a
bewildering maze. The backdrop was the
foothills of the Rockies breaking the skyline
with their snowy peaks and conifer-clad
sides. The westering sun silhouetted the
hills, but lit their tops with gold.

"It's absolutely gorgeous!" Then she clamped her mouth closed. She was trying to reel it in. Emily was always so even-keeled and understated that Chelsea was constantly stumbling to be less...Chelsea. Emily was this perfect woman with a drop-dead handsome husband and about the cutest kid on the planet. Chelsea had only been their daughter's nanny for a few months, but she'd seen the deference and respect that everyone at Mount Hood Aviation's firefighter airbase paid Emily. In return, the woman was kind, courteous, and utterly terrifying. Chelsea wouldn't mind being all of those things.

Her husband Mark, who sat up front in the other pilot seat of the small plane, wasn't much more effusive—except around his daughter. At least he had a sense of humor, though not as much a one as he thought he did; an observation Chelsea kept carefully to herself.

Chelsea looked over at Tessa who was strapped in beside her. She had her tiny version of her mother's elegant nose pressed up against the window. "Green," she announced. Out her window was nothing but the rolling grasslands of eastern Montana.

"It's wrong," Mark agreed solemnly but turned enough to wink at Chelsea, or at least she presumed that's what his cheek twitch was indicating at the lower edge of his mirrored Ray-Bans. "Not much snow in the hills. Means another drought year next summer."

"That's not the problem," Emily responded. "Okay, drought is a problem. But that's not the real problem."

"What is, Emma?" Again the sassy wink that said he already knew what his wife was talking about. It was amazing that the man had survived this long. Chelsea would never dare tease Emily Beale; she could probably kill with a glance if she ever took off her own mirrored shades.

"It's December," Emily took one hand off the plane's wheel—if she was on board, she was the one doing the flying—and waved it helplessly at the stunning scenery before them. "We came to Montana for a white Christmas."

"I thought it was to see Mom and Dad. Make sure Tessa sees them."

"It's still supposed to be white," she grumbled and set up to land the plane. It was as much emotion Chelsea had seen in her entire two months with them. Emily Beale was never unkind, but she was cold. Or at least chilly. But that wasn't right either. The woman was frank and forthright, as much with her daughter as with her husband. Yet Tessa was often in her lap, welcome not as child to adult, but rather as a piece of Emily that was simply back in the place where it belonged. The mother and daughter weren't close; they were simply one when they were together. It was about the most incredible thing Chelsea had ever seen. It made her ache for a family of her own; not a familiar feeling.

Again Chelsea strained up against her seatbelt to look down. A herd of horses startled and looked up at them as they passed by. They didn't scatter and run, but they eyed the low-flying plane carefully.

"Horsies!" Tessa declared delightedly when Emily shifted her flightpath so that the herd was visible outside her daughter's window. Not cold at all, just…inscrutable.

"Yes," Chelsea encouraged the toddler. "Those are horses. Aren't they pretty?"

"Pretty!" Tessa burbled, and they laughed together with delight.

Chelsea had never seen a whole herd of horses before. There were at least fifty in the group of every shade imaginable: grays, browns, whites, blacks, and mixes in patchworks, dapples, and who knew what all. They were gone behind the plane too fast to distinguish more. She tucked away the trail mix snack they'd been sharing to make sure Tessa's blood sugar was up.

Even after two months, Chelsea wasn't quite sure how she'd ended up in this situation. Not that she was complaining, Emily and Mark were great parents and it showed in their total sweetheart of a daughter. And flying with Mark over forest fires was often very dramatic.

It had started with Aunt Betsy who was a cook for the Mount Hood Aviation helicopter and smoke jumping firefighters. When Chelsea's degree in psychology hadn't led to any kind of a useful job, her aunt had asked if she liked to fly. She'd shrugged a yes because she'd flown in passenger jets any number of times to visit grandparents, and a trip to Nepal for a backpacking gap year.

She'd now spent most of the last two months sitting in tiny planes of six or eight narrow seats and been paid to enjoy the scenery and play with a baby girl. Best job she'd ever had by a long way.

Tessa was a fixture in Mark Henderson's plane when he was flying as the Incident Commander high above the fire. What was surprising wasn't that they'd added a nanny, but rather how he'd done the job for so long without one. Tessa was a pretty low maintenance kid, but she was also eighteen months old and quite intelligent.

It was a late fire season, Mark had said, and MHA had still been flying fire in the Southwest. But, finally released from the summer contract, they'd come north for a vacation and brought Chelsea along with them. She sure as hell wasn't going home. They'd known that.

As they flew closer to the ranch, more and more fences became visible, cutting the prairie into smaller pastures and training rings. There were several barns, smaller residences, and cabins surrounding the main residence.

Emily flew once over the grand log-built ranch house and waggled the plane's wings in a friendly wave.

Chelsea pointed to out to Tessa, "Isn't it amazabiling?"

"'mazbling!" Tessa called out happily. Emily sighed audibly as she circled wide of the barn.

Chelsea wondered if Mark's habits were rubbing off on her, but she couldn't resist messing with Tessa's rapidly developing language set. They landed on a gravel strip that ended close beside the house and a large out-building that turned out to be a hangar.

A big man strolled out to meet them, still buttoning up his sheepskin jacket. He was an older version of Mark; just as tall, just as broad-shouldered, his light hair going silver. But Mark's face was different.

Darker, broader, and his hair was thick, straight, and almost midnight black, sharing only his father's gray eyes.

The clouds of mist puffing about with each breath of Mark Senior—Mac, she reminded herself, they'd said he liked to be called Mac—had Chelsea bundling up Tessa before the plane came to a halt in front of a hangar. The ground might be snow free, but it was far colder here than Oregon where they'd boarded the plane.

2

Doug Daniels had stuck his head out of the barn when he heard the plane come over low. The trademark gloss-black-and-red-flame paint job told him who was aboard. Some part of him had been alarmed that a client was in-bound for a ranch vacation even though they hadn't taken any Christmas reservations this year. But it was just Mark and his knock-out wife. He liked Mark fine, but he had trouble speaking around Emily Beale. It wasn't just the beauty, he knew how to talk to pretty women just fine; it was the fierce level of competence that she demonstrated at every turn.

He finished helping Logan pitch the hay into the stalls' feedboxes before heading out to greet them. The air had a sharp bite to it, wholly different from the horse-and-straw of the barn, but no moisture. As he stepped out of the barn, he noticed that there wasn't even a hint of cloud in the cobalt blue of the late afternoon sky. The temperature was already dropping though it was still an hour to sunset. It was going to get cold tonight.

Doug stuck his head back inside. "Hey, Logan. Open up the gates. If the main herd has any sense, they'll be coming this way by sunset."

"You bet, boss. Any horse that stays out there tonight needs his horse-sense meter checked."

Doug went out to help stow the plane. There was room in the hangar because he'd moved the helicopter tight to the side after the morning's flight to check the main herd and make sure there were no stray or injured. He hadn't been able to get an accurate count, but it had felt low and that was bothering him. Happened all the time. Still, it worried him.

He ducked through the hangar's side door, popped the release, and slid open the main door from the inside. It rattled and boomed in the cold air. A sharp squeal in one of the wheels had him adding "needs grease" to the infinite mental checklist that was running a working dude ranch.

Just emerging from the plane was a figure wrapped deep in a parka, with the fur-rimmed hood already raised as if it wasn't a merely brisk day, but rather a north polar night. She, for there was no chance of a guy wearing such tight jeans and making them look so good, carried an equally bundled child.

He came up and stuck his nose right into the child's hood, "Tessa, my love! Give us a kiss!"

"Kiss!" the little girl squealed and kissed him on the nose.

Then he rubbed noses with her until she was giggling before he pulled back. He'd ended up standing very close to the woman holding her. He could just see brilliant blue eyes, a freckled nose, and a bright smile in the narrow opening of the hood.

"Do you greet all the girls that way?" Her tone was light, almost musical.

"Sure." Never one to back down from a challenge, he stuck his face right into her hood until their noses rubbed and cried out, "Give us a kiss!"

Unlike the little girl, there was no squeal. Instead, there was a quick squawk of surprise.

Way over the line, Doug.

But before he could retreat, she gave him a quick kiss. Unlike Tessa's it didn't land on his nose, but right on the mouth. There and gone, but the lips were warm, soft, and tasted of peanuts and chocolate.

Once he was clear of the hood, the gloved slap that he expected to follow, didn't. He glanced again into the tunnel of the raised hood.

The bright blue eyes caught the low sunlight and weren't round with shock or narrowed with anger.

"Well," she blinked in slow motion, "okay then."

He laughed, he couldn't help himself.

Now that was his kind of woman.

3

Chelsea had no idea what had come over her. She didn't randomly kiss men, even tall handsome ones who adored small children.

Men who then scooped a little girl out of her arms, slung her around with the ease of long practice until she was riding piggy-back, and—while Tessa shouted, "Horsie!" with glee—galloped about the yard with a protective hand wrapped awkwardly behind him. The man shook back his collar-length, sun-streaked hair the color of worn leather so that it brushed in Tessa's face. He let out a fierce whinny escalating her giggles of delight.

He trotted up to Mark and Emily then stopped with a sidle and a stomp that was thoroughly horselike and delivered the child to Emily. Then he and Mark made quick work of pushing the plane back into the hangar.

Chelsea was still standing shocked into place when they'd finished and the men had returned carrying the luggage.

"A field pack, very practical," the man who'd kissed her held it aloft as if it contained only air rather than most of Chelsea's worldly belongings. Her camping gear was stashed at Aunt Betsy's and a dozen boxes of books at Mom and Dad's, but the rest of it was in that pack.

"It's my hiking pack, but I use it for everything. Really practical since I hike a lot," she was rambling; time to cut that out. She sniffed at the air and the cold made her nose hurt on the insides, "At least when it isn't sub-Arctic."

The man's jacket was fleeced-line denim, but he hadn't even bothered to button it against the frosty day. He smelled of hay and his kiss had been warm and fresh with the outdoors.

Mac greeted his son with a firm handshake, but gave Emily a deep hug that surprised Chelsea almost as much as being kissed by a total stranger. What had happened to the woman's backbone of steel? Emily leaned into Mac's hug as if she was the one related by blood and was happily come home. Then he led them toward the house, leaving Chelsea and her luggage bearer to trail behind.

"Do you have a name or should I just shout 'Sherpa!' when I want your attention? Or perhaps *daai?*"

"*Daai?*" he led her onto the wide porch and held the door for her to enter the mud room. There they shed boots and jackets. She was glad she'd been wearing a thick sweater against the damp chill in Oregon and kept it on for added warmth.

The others were talking happily enough together to be lost in their own conversation as they too stripped off the outdoor gear and pulled on slippers from the large basketful of them close by the inner door.

"*Daai* means *older brother* in Nepalese," she explained softly. "A sign of respect. Better yet, *bhaai* for *younger brother* as who knows if you're worthy of respect."

"You kiss me and question whether I'm worth respecting? That doesn't bode well for the morning after."

Chelsea was preparing a comeback, for she certainly wasn't the one who had done the kissing…or had she been, when she turned and saw the look on his face.

"What?"

He shook himself like a horse again. "If I'd known what was under that hood, I might have spent longer kissing you."

"Skin deep, *bhaai.*"

"Yes, but what a nice layer it is."

4

Doug knew he was staring, but how was a man supposed to not? Thick waves of red hair cascaded down to her shoulders. Her cream-and-freckle skin only highlighted the brilliant blue eyes that were presently rolling at him. Her sweater must have been custom-made because it traced and enhanced the slender woman within. The rich green was finished with red zig-zags at wrists and waist. A small but elegant snowflake had been knit right over her heart.

"Frozen heart?" He teased to hide his suddenly dry throat.

She looked down where his attention had strayed. "I called this one White Christmas, *bhaai*. And watch where you're looking."

"I am watching where I'm looking, and very glad to be doing so," his made his voice pure tease. Then he wondered, "You name your sweaters?" Could he sound much stupider?

"Sure. At least the Christmas ones."

"You knit it yourself?" Apparently yes, he could sound dumber. But there was something about this girl—woman. She *liked* hiking? Major understatement. Her pack looked like it had been carried by an entire Army brigade, worn shiny in a hundred places. A very well-used piece of top quality gear. She knew terms of respect in Nepalese and could knit sweaters that made her look like a Christmas delight.

"I—" they stepped out of the mud room and into the living room. Her gasp of amazement echoed that of all who came here. Every ranch guest who entered the main house couldn't help but stumble to a halt.

"Quite something, isn't it?"

"It's gorgeous! A little daunting, but…" she did a slow twirl to take it all in. "But this is right out of a magazine. It's unbelievable!"

The large river-stone fireplace was a showpiece, big double-length logs crackled away on the grate. The flagstone hearth was surrounded by plush chairs and inviting sofas. An upright piano stood by a corner window overlooking the horse pastures and snow-capped peaks. And the high-beamed cathedral ceiling made the twelve-foot spruce that he and Mac had felled up on the northwest slope fit right in. The Hendersons always really did up Christmas. Coils of holly were draped from mantel and piano. Wreaths, garlands, winter-themed quilts on the walls…

"Quite the spectacle, isn't it?" And this nameless woman in a sweater named White Christmas fit right in.

"It's fabulous! My family does a totally lame Christmas, as in almost not at all. Once I got to college, I discovered it and turned into the Christmas loon of any group. You should have seen this poor pistachio tree I decorated on year in Puri."

"Puri?"

"India. On the east coast. I spent a couple months traveling there by train after I left the Himalayas."

Himalayas? Right, well, that explained where she'd picked up the Nepalese. What hadn't she done?

"I try to do up my place, too," he answered. "Same style of construction, but cozier. Bet you'd like it too."

"You do, huh?" Something was amusing her but he couldn't quite think what.

"Sure. I live on the far side of the meadow. I'm the ranch foreman."

"Your…place."

"They gave me a sweet little setup. Two bedrooms. Looks a lot like this, just on a smaller scale. A ranch house in miniature."

"You bet I'd like it?" Her tone had gone impossibly dry.

And her meaning finally sunk through his thick skull. "I didn't mean—" He'd just invited a woman whose name he still didn't know back to his place for a quick—

Someone should just take him out to pasture and shoot him.

A wicked smile crossed her features. "Sure know how to make a girl feel welcome, *bhaai.*"

Little brother. Suddenly that really wasn't the role he wanted to be cast in. Not even a little. Because he could certainly picture her clearly in that cozy little log house of his.

5

Chelsea was curled up in one of the big chairs by the fire with Tessa on her lap. The girl was fading, but not out yet and Chelsea felt completely content working through the thousandth iteration of *Carl's Snowy Afternoon* picture book.

Mark's parents were relaxing comfortably in side-by-side armchairs. It was easy to see where Mark had gotten his good looks. His father had passed on his physique and kindly eyes. His mother Ama was half Cheyenne and had passed on dark skin and hair to her son.

The three of them together were stunning.

Mark sat on an oak-trimmed leather couch and Emily was curled up against him with a woven throw of geometric tans and dark reds across her legs. She looked as sleepy as their daughter while the others talked about the ranch, and fires that MHA had flown to this season. Tessa had her father's gray eyes and her mother's fine features and blond beauty. When Tessa was grown, the three of them would make an equally stunning trio.

It was so unusual to see Emily relaxed, that it made Chelsea content to remain as long as she could in the room. Emily, the successful senior helicopter pilot of Mount Hood Aviation, the woman always in absolute control of any situation, lying against her husband like…well, like a woman in love. It was surprising and wonderful. Yet another thing that Chelsea put into her Someday List. Lie before a warm fire with her arms wrapped around a man she loved.

No. Scratch that. With *the* man she loved. She still had plenty of time to find him; she hoped. Mr. Wonderfuls weren't exactly hanging about for the picking, but it was a nice image.

It wasn't hard to picture what the man would look like in her fire-warmed daydream. He'd have casually long rough-cut hair, worn-leather brown just like—

There was a soft jolt in her lap. She looked down to see that Tessa had landed face first and fast asleep with her nose on Carl's finished snowman.

Chelsea slipped from the room with her and decided that it was time to put both Tessa and herself to bed before she became any more ridiculous.

Still, it was a nice image as she curled up in a guest room with Tessa on a low trundle bed beside her.

Doug Daniels was a *very* nice image.

6

"Can't sleep all day, c'mon."

Doug went for brash to cover his initial reaction to seeing a sleep-tousled Chelsea hunched at the breakfast table. He'd come in to refill his coffee and check up on her as Emily had asked. It looked as if he'd surprised the sleeping lion in her den.

Wrong image. Chelsea didn't strike him as dangerous, just enthusiastic. Like an Irish Setter. The dark red hair color wasn't a bad match. Except at the moment she looked like she'd been run over by warm bed and a soft pillow, and would still be a while recovering. Or like he'd want to sweep her right back into—

Cut it out, Daniels. But he'd lost a lot of sleep over her last night and her current state wasn't helping matters.

Chelsea was clutching a mug of hot chocolate like a lifeline. She wore a gold-colored turtleneck that proved the sweater hadn't lied last night. It revealed strength aplenty to carry a hiking pack and curves to…

He sighed at his libido's nudge-nudge, wink-wink.

"Where's Tessa?" she looked up at him through a screen of unkempt hair that she didn't bother to brush aside. The ten-foot distance from the coffee pot to where he could brush it aside himself was a good thing.

"They all went into town; took her with."

"I should wait for them."

"They won't be back until dinnertime."

She squinted up at him again. "Where the heck is town from here?"

"Highfalls is only thirty miles out, but there's not much there unless you fancy a good steak. They're headed into Great Falls which is eighty each way."

"You sure?"

"There's a note from Emily by your elbow."

She twisted her head to read it without relaxing the death grip on her mug. The long line of her neck was…something he shouldn't be thinking about. Mark and Emily might not be his bosses, but this was their guest. And thinking hot thoughts about Tessa's nanny was wrong in so many ways, not the least of it being that they'd be gone soon. Christmas was just the day after tomorrow; they'd be gone the next day.

"You eaten yet?"

She nodded.

It took him a moment to spot the pan and dish, already washed and perched in the drying rack. Neat and respectful too.

"Good. Dress warmly. I'll meet you at the hangar in five minutes. I need to go up."

"Or I could just kill you and go back to my cozy bed."

"You'd do that to *younger brother?*" he asked in horror.

"Absolutely," but he could hear the grin in her voice even if he couldn't see it clearly through her shield of hair.

"You'll miss a beautiful helicopter ride."

"*You* know how to fly one?" She was quick enough to take in that he must be the pilot and turn it around into a tease.

He didn't even condescend to answer as he headed for the back door. "Four and a half minutes."

7

Chelsea made it in four and had spent three of that whipping up some instant hot chocolate in a pair of steel travel mugs.

"For me? Thanks."

When he reached for one, she pulled it away. "Mine. Two-fisted drinker."

It earned her that good laugh of his and she handed one over.

Doug had a pretty little Bell JetRanger pulled out of the hangar and was going over it carefully. Chelsea was taken aback for a moment. Two months ago she knew helicopters were the ones with their propellers on top instead of pointing to the front; now she recognized a JetRanger on sight. Furthermore, she thought of it as small compared to the massive Firehawk helicopter that Emily flew for MHA. When had that happened to her?

The pilot-plus-four-passenger craft was clean, but well worn. It looked well-maintained but hard used.

"I've never flown in a helicopter."

Doug looked at her aghast. "You work for two of the best helicopter pilots the Army has ever produced and you haven't been up in one?"

"I—" Chelsea hadn't known that about them. But rather than look foolish for the lack of knowledge, she just shrugged. "My job is to take care of Tessa. Mark is the Incident Commander Air"—she hadn't even known he could *fly* a helicopter—"so I fly with him and Tessa in the ICA plane."

"A helicopter virgin. Well, you're in for a thrill, honey."

"Watch it, *bhaai!*"

Again the merry laugh as he escorted her into the left-hand seat and buckled her in.

The ride was a real joy. The cabin heater kept the chill air at bay as they roared aloft. Headsets with boom mics made it easy to hear him as he pointed out the features of the ranch.

He let her look her fill, but she didn't know if she'd ever get enough. The green prairie stretched smoothly to the hills. The mountains broke from the grassland as if someone had drawn a line on the ground and said, "start them here." It was an abrupt and visceral shock. Only as they flew closer did the illusion start to break; secluded valleys intruded deep into the hills with small rivers sliding between sheer headlands.

"I love this land," Doug whispered softly after she'd finally managed to voice her awe at the rugged beauty. "It can be a hard land, but I never tire of looking at it."

"I wouldn't either," she said with a sincerity as if she was making a promise.

"Now who's being forward?"

She hadn't meant to be. Then she realized that she hadn't been. It was just Doug Daniel's mind twisting in…she sighed… much the way hers had been.

But the ranch was one of those places that simply felt right. Chelsea would start helicopter lessons tomorrow if it meant she could fly here. Doug flew with such an easy confidence.

"You've been flying for a long time," she finally turned her attention to the fine scenery inside the cabin.

"Navy. Did three tours, six years. That was enough for me and then some. A SEAL buddy hooked me up with Mac."

"A SEAL buddy? Like the diver guys?"

"Sure, Mac was one too," Doug shrugged easily. No wonder he flew with such ease and confidence. Except he didn't look confident; he looked worried.

"What's wrong?" She checked the narrow dashboard that rose on a pedestal between their feet. She recognized about half of the instruments that were like the ones in Mark's plane, but nothing looked wrong on them and nothing was flashing red.

"Lucy didn't come back to the barn last night. And she had a late season foal, so I'm a little worried about them."

Chelsea looked out the windshield but couldn't imagine how to spot a horse in such a vast area. Now at least she understood that Doug hadn't been sweeping back and forth over the ranch and the prairie simply to show it to her; he'd been quartering and searching the ground. She'd done search and rescue for lost hikers, but that was tromping through woods and over rough terrain.

"How do you find a horse in thousands of acres?"

"Well," he pointed down at a lush, pocket-sized meadow around a tiny lake. "I was hoping she'd be here. It's a favorite of the horses. Hold the collective a minute."

"The what?"

"The control on the left side of your seat. Just hold it steady, don't worry, you can't crash us."

She tentatively wrapped her hand around the control, until she had a firm grasp. "Okay," she barely dared whisper it.

Doug took his left hand off his matching control and reached back to scrabble around behind the seat.

Daring greatly, she pulled up on it ever so slightly, and could feel the helicopter rise. She eased back down until the altimeter said she was back at the starting level.

"Here," he dropped something heavy in her lap. "Put that on, would you?"

She opened the case and looked down at the contraption, for that was the only word for it. There were straps to hold it to your head. It looked like a pair of goggles from one side, and like a half-unicorn, half-bug-eyed monster monocular protruding from the other.

"What is it?"

"Night vision. Lucy and the foal will be significantly warmer than the background. She'll show up clearly. Mark gets us the best toys."

Chelsea straightened it out and leaned over to put it on Doug's head.

"No," he stopped her. "You wear it."

8

Doug was amused by her exclamation when she got it turned on. Chelsea took such pleasure from everything about her. The countryside, the helicopter—rather than showing fear she'd proved she had a good and light touch—and now the night vision was tickling her fancy. Last night he'd left early. Partly because it was a time for the family to be together, but also because the vision of Chelsea with Tessa in her lap had been so powerful. She'd made it too easy to imagine a red-headed girl sitting right there, curled up by his fireplace.

For the next two hours, he flew and she scanned. He filled the time with learning about her background. Deeply independent—with parents who had little interest in an intelligent child filled with dreams—she'd forged out on her own. Six years to get her degree because she'd spent two years traveling and hiking; first walking the Continental Divide Trail from New Mexico to Glacier Park, and then all over the Himalayas.

It both amazed and saddened him. She was incredible, had a much clearer view of the world and herself than most people. But he'd found where he wanted to be and she had adventure deep in her blood. She'd never be satisfied with…stupid fantasies of a demented ranch manager.

"There," her shriek almost blew his eardrums. Close beside the farthest fishing cabin, Lucy and her foal were huddled up against the side of the building. Lucy was lying down. Not a good sign.

He landed as close as he dared and rushed out to the mare. He'd brought a handgun, but not wanting to jar Chelsea's sensibilities, he'd left it stowed on the helo.

"We won't have to shoot her, will we?" Chelsea was right beside him.

Okay, so much for that worry. "Let's hope not."

Lucy was down, but had raised her head to watch his approach. Her whinny of greeting was encouraging.

He talked to her as he checked her out. No complaints as he tested for broken limbs. Same for the abdomen. Then she coughed in his face, a dry, hacking cough. He felt under her jaw and found swollen lymph nodes.

"Oh, crap!"

"What?"

"We vaccinated her against this."

"What?" Chelsea sounded deeply worried.

He sighed, "She has the flu. I can't do much for her here. She needs a warm barn and some rest. I'll have to ride back out, bring some high energy food and probably start her on a round antibiotics against secondary infection. With a little luck, she'll come back if I guide her. It will be a long slow ride."

9

They flew back, and when Doug saddled up a horse, she'd insisted he saddle two. She'd never ridden a horse, only a very recalcitrant mule when she'd sprained an ankle coming off climbing Imja Tse. She could have hobbled out faster than that Nepalese mule had carried her.

At Doug's guidance, she'd packed a pair of saddlebags with a change of clothes and several days of food. He packed clothes, camping gear in case they were caught out, horse meds, and a twenty pound sack of oats.

He led off at a light trot and she let him. Her horse, a big dapple gray male called Snowflake, looked at her strangely several times as she struggled to imitate Doug's easy saddle position. Every now and then he'd glance back to make sure she was still with him, and she always managed a plucky wave or nod as the saddle's hard leather slowly beat her to death.

They were about an hour out when he happened to look back during one of her barely-still-on-the-horse moments. Doug twisted his mount in a tight circle like it was the easiest thing in the world. He twisted again until they were side by side. He leaned over to grab Snowflake's reins and everything came to a blessed halt.

"Haven't you ridden before?"

She could only shake her head, because if she opened her mouth she might start crying from all the places she'd rubbed raw.

"You're either incredibly brave or ridiculously stupid!"

"Mostly," she managed through gritted teeth. "Except you got the adjectives backwards." Being at a blessed standstill gave her some tiny sliver of ease. "According to my parents, I'm ridiculously brave and incredibly stupid."

Doug regarded her for a long moment, then glanced in both the direction they'd come and the one they were headed, considering the options. If he tried to send her back, she'd…she didn't know what. But she hadn't gone through this much pain for nothing.

"Okay," he shook his head. "I've seen that look on plenty a stubborn horse and don't want an argument. Stand up in your stirrups, if you still can."

She managed it without crying out.

He unrolled an extra blanket he'd had tied to the back of his saddle. He folded it in quarters, tossed it over her saddle, and then pressed her lightly on the shoulder until she eased back down carefully. It wasn't too painful, and far better than it had been.

"I lead probably a hundred trail rides a summer, Chelsea. You know how many beginner riders could have pulled off what you just did?"

She shook her head.

He held up his fingers and thumb, tips together to show a zero.

"I deserve a prize then."

Chelsea only had a moment to see his grin before he leaned in and kissed her. This wasn't some quick peck through the shield of her parka.

Doug leaned into the kiss and, fool that she was, she welcomed it without even a little protest. He provided plenty skill and heat, but that wasn't what she was really noticing. What riveted her attention was how absolutely her body was galvanized by the simple act. Actually, ungalvanized. She melted against him despite the two horses that separated them. Leaning as far as she dared, she hung tightly onto the saddle's pommel with one hand and his jacket with the other and pulled them together. The kiss ran right down to her toes and made them curl in her riding boots.

When he finally eased back, Doug Daniels looked awfully pleased with himself. Of course she was feeling much the same way.

"I'm not sure," Chelsea was amazed she could even speak, "which of us you were just rewarding."

"At least you won't be *bhaai-ing* me any more," his laugh was even more self-satisfied than his expression. "Now, let's teach you how to ride. First, take your reins like this."

She did her best to follow his instructions and pay attention, but he'd made a warm buzz between her ears despite the cool day only now breaking above freezing.

Doug Daniels was many things: handsome, male, and a heavenly kisser being only three of them. But *younger brother* he definitely wasn't.

10

It was four hours to the last turn up to the fishing cabin, less than an hour later than he'd planned. Chelsea was the most apt riding student he'd ever taught, and while Henderson Ranch might be a working one, they made the majority of their income from all of the city folk guests who wanted a week or two of "country." Chelsea took to it as if she'd been born in the saddle... though she'd probably be too stiff to walk right for days. It had been cruel to keep going, but he couldn't afford the time to escort her back even if she'd have let him.

He'd bet the chances of that were close to zero, yet another thing to appreciate about the beautiful woman. Tenacious as hell.

As it was, they'd be staying in the fishing cabin tonight. The sunset was only a few hours off and Lucy wouldn't be able to move quickly. It would be a far slower ride back tomorrow. On top of that, keeping Chelsea in the saddle through the night's journey back would be a cruelty, even if Lucy was up to it.

The final lap to the cabin at their quick walk should take about half an hour. Then Doug glanced back over his shoulder— more bad news. A squall was inbound. Blocked by the height of Wind Mountain, and the twisting trail up to the cabin, he hadn't seen it coming. He stopped them long enough to haul on ponchos, but he knew it wouldn't be enough. They were about to get drenched.

They'd galloped briefly on the flat trail, but they were now climbing up a harder route. The way wasn't dangerously narrow, but it would be far more challenging. Another eye at the rain front, now a gray curtain sliding down the mountain face, had him changing plans.

"Ease up out of the saddle a little bit," he told Chelsea. "Lean forward. Loosen the rein. Good!"

And he smacked Snowflake hard on the butt.

He nudged his own mount forward and in moments they were galloping together up the valley. The way narrowed and steepened until they could no longer ride side by side. Doug didn't dare lead from where he couldn't see her.

"Ride on!" he shouted as the first crash of lightning struck the mountain top and thunder rumbled down upon them, amplified by the echoes off the high rock cliffs.

Bless Chelsea, she leaned into it and flew up the trail. He watched closely, but she stayed solid, didn't even a grab the pommel. Her legs must be screaming fire, but she rode, if not like an experienced horsewoman, then plenty close.

The icy rain broke over them, but the trail was solid and drained well, so he left them at the run.

In five minutes they were drenched, but the cabin was in sight. He shouted ahead and they eased down through canter to trot and arrived at the cabin at a walk.

"Down you go," he slid off and helped her down from her horse. "Take their reins and walk them back and forth. It will do all three of you good. Slow is fine, just keep moving." He stripped the saddle bags and tossed them into the cabin. He heaved the saddles inside moments later, then waved her, holding their mounts' reins, down the valley.

Even aching and saddle sore the woman had a walk that stirred his blood. *Ridiculous!* That's what he was being.

He grabbed his medicine bag and the oats and circled around to Lucy who was thankfully back on her feet, but hanging her head miserably in the rain. Her foal was cowering against her. She'd been ten feet from the overhang and the big box stall, but had been too dazed—yet another symptom—to walk under cover.

He guided them in and checked her. He couldn't do anything for the flu, which was viral, but he gave her antibiotics against secondary infection and a booster shot of vitamins. She perked up a bit for her oats and water. He got blankets over her and the foal about the time Chelsea staggered back up to the stall with their mounts plodding along behind her.

"Is this enough?"

He ran a hand over them. No longer breathing hard, not hot. "You did good Chelsea. Go inside. I'll be in as soon as I get these two settled with the mare."

When he entered the cabin a few minutes later, Chelsea was on the floor in a fetal position.

Shit! He was an idiot.

11

Chelsea had been this cold before, she was sure of it. Like when she'd camped above snowline at the base of Chulu West and the zipper on her sleeping bag had broken. But in her memory it didn't feel colder. And when her knees had knocked together high in the Himalayas, she'd laughed at the novelty. Now she fought not to cry as the insides of her legs, rubbed raw by the saddle, sent shivers of pain right along with the cold shakes.

She opened her eyes when Doug entered the cabin and immediately began cursing.

He looked furious! His dark hair matted flat and black with the rain, water cascading off his poncho. He hauled it off with a yank and dropped it on the rough wood with a wet splat.

Chelsea wondered if he was about to tear her to shreds because she'd collapsed, then realized she wasn't the one he was swearing at. He dropped to his knees beside her and began calling her name loudly.

"I'm c-c-c-cold, not d-d-deaf," she managed through rattling teeth.

"I'll start a fire," he jumped up toward the iron woodstove in the corner.

She tried avoiding the hard "c" of close, but found the "sh" sound little easier. "Sh-sh-shut the door first, you big lummox. R-raised in a b-b-barn."

Doug closed the door and then re-deemed himself with his efficiency in building the fire.

"Heat? How long?" she managed.

He looked uncertainly from her to the stove. Not soon enough.

She tried to remove her poncho, but her hands weren't under her control anymore.

This was bad.

"C-c-clothes. Off. B-b-bed," she instructed.

He stripped off the outer layers and hesitated until she stuttered out a series of curses at him. She cried out when he peeled her jeans.

Then he began cursing all over again.

She looked down. Her legs' normally pale skin had gone white with the cold, except for the insides from boot top to panties were livid red with abrasions. No wonder they hurt.

The goofball stopped at her soaking wet turtleneck as if embarrassed.

"C-c-come on. You know you want to s-s-see me naked."

He grunted and had the decency to try and look away as he finished the job and then scooped her up like a feather hard against his soaking wet jacket.

"Eww!" Yet even the tiny bit of heat that escaped through the denim felt so good.

The cabin was simple. Three bunk beds, several couches and plush chairs that had seen better days probably back at the main house, and a small corner kitchen with an impressive collection of cast iron pans appropriate for frying fish. Doug dropped her in one of the lower bunks and began piling blankets over her. She couldn't even clutch the blankets to pull them tighter.

"S-s-strip!" Chelsea ordered.

"But…"

"C-c-come on. You know I want to s-s-see you naked," she did her best to stammer it out the same way she had the first time. "I need heat."

He began peeling down and Chelsea watched as much as the shivers would allow.

"Wow! C-c-cowboys *are* built pretty."

He smiled at her for the first time since finding her on the floor. "This is a horse ranch. Not a cattle ranch."

"So get your fine butt in here, horseboy. Before I f-f-freeze to death."

He hesitated at shedding his underwear, someone please explain men to her, then turned away as he finally stripped off that last piece. His butt really was fine; topped by a narrow waist and broad shoulders with muscle that rippled across them with each movement.

Doug slid in beside her and, after a moment's hesitation, pulled her against him. His skin was so warm compared to hers that it burned, but she leaned into it as hard as she could.

"Christ! You're freezing!" He began chaffing those big hands of his up and down her back.

"D-d-duh!" Chelsea managed to get the covers completely over her head and concentrated on soaking up Doug Daniels' warmth.

12

Doug held her until the shivers stopped.
With his arms still around her, he could feel
her breathing slow. Once she was deeply
asleep in exhaustion, he slipped out of
bed and dug out fresh clothes from the
saddlebags, hanging the others to dry. He
stoked the fire, made hot chocolate and
wished for coffee, but the latter would make
him even more awake than he already was.

A quick radio call back to Logan told
him that the Hendersons weren't back from
Great Falls yet. Logan wasn't a pilot so he
couldn't bring the helo to fetch Chelsea.

With the shakes gone, she probably just needed sleep…and time to heal. Gods but she was tough.

The windows were dark with the fading light of sunset happening somewhere beyond the heavy overcast. Lightning still shimmered through the heavy rain, though far enough off that the thunder was a rumble rather than a crack. The weather was still too nasty for a flight even if Mark was back. He had Logan leave a message on the kitchen table so that they wouldn't worry when they returned and found no Chelsea.

"Doug," Chelsea's voice was a whisper barely louder than the crackling flame from the glass-fronted woodstove. "Come back to bed." The firelight caught the blue of her eyes and the tip of her nose from where they peeked out of the blankets.

"You trying to kill me, girl?" Yes, he'd wanted to see Chelsea naked, from the first moment he'd spotted her climbing down out of that plane in those deliciously tight jeans. Even shuddering with the leading edge of hypothermia, she was beyond spectacular.

"Not girl. It's woman. And I think you trying to kill me once already today should be enough for both of us."

"I didn't—" But he had. He'd taken her skills for granted when she climbed up on the horse. And led her on a grueling ride through a storm. Sending her out on a cool-down walk in the freezing rain was about as dumb as it got.

Unlike so many of the guests who came to the ranch, Chelsea radiated skill. She'd triggered none of his high-season alarms that told him who to watch out for. Though she was certainly triggering other reactions.

"I don't think that's a good idea."

She rolled her eyes at him. "Get your warm butt back in here before I have to climb out and kick it. I ache right down to my joints."

Which told him just how dangerously cold she'd gotten.

Once again he stripped down, far more conscious of the woman who now wouldn't turn away than the earlier one whose eyes had been partly rolled back into her head.

She went to throw a leg over his, but jerked back and hissed at the pain.

"God I'm so sorry. Let me get some horse liniment," he climbed out of the bunk.

"Hello! Not a horse."

He grabbed a bottle from the kitchen shelf and returned to stand over the bed. How was he supposed to…

"Here," he held out the bottle. "Trust me. It works great."

13

Chelsea felt as if she was being a total
wanton. She was in a cozy little cabin
with no distractions of electricity. A very
handsome man, momentarily unaware of
his own nakedness, stood close beside her
lit by the soft firelight that filtered through
the woodstove's glass-paned door. And he
was holding out the horse liniment the way
you hold out a mouse for a dangerous viper
to snack on.

The normal version of herself would
have taken the liniment and tried to slather
it on under the covers.

Instead, she watched Doug's face as she slipped a leg out from under the covers and twisted to turn it, inside-thigh up. His eyes didn't narrow suspiciously, instead they widened in alarm. She'd watched him handling the horses with a gentle but firm hand. A half ton of horse flesh didn't bother him at all, but the inside of a woman's leg had him totally flustered. Damn but he was cute.

"Come along, horseboy," she coaxed him in the same tone he'd cajoled the colt to follow its mother into the stall.

His gaze snapped from her leg to her face, and then his nice deep laugh rolled out. "Okay, you got me. I'm dying to slather some liniment on those fine legs of yours." And he knelt on the wood floor beside her and smoothed some on.

It was cold and sent a shiver up her leg. But the warm steadiness of his hand stroking in the thick liquid calmed the convulsive response before it could turn back into the shakes. She could feel his hard calluses and easy strength, but was surprised at the gentleness of his rough hands. Within moments a numbing warmth spread up her leg in a wave of relief.

"I'll smell like a horse," she complained to cover a moan of delight. The camphor was sharp in the cabin's warm air, but her attention was nowhere near her nose.

"A sweet smell to a rancher."

"How about to a horseboy?"

"Lady," he didn't even bat an eye. "You smell incredible to this horseboy, with or without the liniment."

There was no sign of any embarrassment by the time he'd ministered to both her legs and tucked them once more under the covers. He'd somehow transferred all of it to her. As he slid back under the layers of blankets, Chelsea was intensely aware of the narrow bunk and the warmth of his body pressed against hers. She was more of a long t-shirt gal, but it would be stupid to ask for one with a man she'd lain naked against for most of the last few hours.

Unable to find words, she simply nestled inside the curve of his arm. Then, against the fiery tension building so high that it roared in her ears, Doug began talking. He told her about the birth of the foal, who slept even now in the nearby stall with Lucy. He talked about the ranch and the spring wildflowers that colored the prairie like a paintbrush.

She fell asleep with the sound of his love for his life rumbling from his chest directly into her ear. It was the sweetest, safest sound she'd ever heard.

14

He'd offered to call the helo a half dozen times this morning, but Chelsea had turned him down cold, despite hobbling about like a geriatric case. Another round of liniment helped some, but he knew she'd be stiff for days.

Doug finally gave in. Partly because he knew Lucy wouldn't be up for more than a casual amble and partly because he wanted every single minute with Chelsea that he could get. He'd held her throughout the night, marveling at the rightness of it.

It had been like that when he'd arrived at the ranch fresh out of the service. After three full tours, most of them spent on ships in the Persian Gulf, he'd been sick to his heart of the unending heat, the limitless steel, and the noise—for a Navy ship was never silent. He'd been on the ranch for three years now and could still feel the Persian dust in his pores. But the ranch had fit him since the first moment he'd stepped on the soil.

He'd ridden plenty as a kid at his parents' place in Wyoming. When he didn't re-up, SEAL Commander Luke Altman had sent him up to see his own former commander outside Highfalls, Montana. Mac had shown him around Henderson Ranch and Doug had decided on the spot that he never wanted to leave. Mac and Ama had been looking for a foreman. Together, they'd transformed the aging ranch into a showplace tourist destination.

He'd worried a lot about "the son" coming home, until he'd met Mark and Emily. Mark had taken one look at the transformation and thumped him hard on the shoulder before walking away without a word.

It was Emily who'd translated for him. "He was so worried for his parents. You've really touched him." Then she'd kissed him on either cheek. "You done good, Doug. Keep it up." Then she'd gone after her husband. That's when he'd set his sights on the kind of woman he wanted. One just like Emily Beale.

And he couldn't have found one more different than Chelsea Bridges if he'd tried. Oh, a lot of the things that were right with Emily were just as right on Chelsea, especially her absolute fearlessness— the image of her galloping through a thunderstorm on her first ride still fired the imagination.

But where Emily was quiet, thoughtful, and soft spoken, Chelsea spoke her mind and laughed with a bright joy—even when on the verge of succumbing to hypothermia.

He imagined it would take years to fall for the right woman once he met her, because his ideal woman didn't fall that quickly. At least so he'd thought until he'd rubbed noses with Chelsea inside a parka hood and received a kiss for it. Now he was crazy about a sassy redhead who'd slept in his arms like she'd always been there.

Slept. And that was all she'd done. Hard to blame her, as her body had been through a lot of extremes yesterday. But the only extremes he'd been through had been treating Chelsea as if she was his injured sister. Everything had been perfectly chaste last night, if you didn't include his thoughts.

"Storm has passed," he did his best to distract himself. "Temperature is falling and there's another front moving in. Let's get ahead of it."

"Sure," she gamely picked up her saddle, that probably weighed half as much as she did, and headed for the door.

So much for a morning tumble, or even a kiss.

He'd escaped her bed early—because it was either that or he was going to do something wholly inappropriate—and bundled up to go tend the horses. Lucy had perked up overnight enough to greet him. She was still snotty with the flu, but it was clear so no secondary infection yet. Her breathing also sounded clear enough for the walk back to the ranch. The foal was more cheerful than the night before, which he'd take as a good sign regarding his mother's condition. By the time he was back inside, Chelsea was dressed in warm clothes and had made the bed. Oatmeal and coffee were simmering on the woodstove.

She'd looked as natural here as no paying guest ever really did.

They'd had breakfast together; Chelsea going on about the upcoming ride…and he hadn't jumped her. What was up with that? There was decent and there was ridiculous, and he'd definitely crossed that line somewhere in the night.

Then she'd washed the dishes, grabbed her saddle, and gone.

He'd already taken his own saddle out. So, he gathered up their saddle bags, double-checked that the woodstove was secure—the few remaining embers would burn themselves out—and gave the cabin one last look. All shipshape…damn it. Not a single tousled bed sheet. He hadn't brought any protection with him, but that didn't mean there weren't other options. But had they used them? Nope! Not a single, damned, inappropriately pleasant fondle had passed between them.

Closing the door, he stomped around to the horse stall and ran head on into a kiss.

This wasn't some little kiss through a parka or a taste of wonder when they were both up on horses. Chelsea wrapped herself around him and had him backed against the rail fence. With her arms tight around his neck, she was rapidly killing off fantasy after fantasy. Who knew it was possible to pack so much joy into such a simple act? Apparently Chelsea did.

When Snowflake came over to snort in his hair across the fence, Chelsea flapped a hand at the horse's nose.

"Busy here," she mumbled at the big gray.

Damn straight! was all Doug could think. All that soft and gentle warmth of last night had been replaced by the lively redhead who'd teased with him since the moment of her arrival. She didn't play coy or tease now; she delivered a kiss with her entire body. It left him shuddering with need when she abruptly released him and, as if his world hadn't just been spun around and dropped on its head, strode into the stall with one of the saddlebags that he'd dropped when she'd jumped him.

Unable to trust his voice, he focused on saddling them up. No need to rope Lucy or the foal. Lucy, he knew would follow them, and the foal would follow his mom.

Placing his hands around Chelsea's waist to help her up into the saddle was almost his undoing. With her arms raised to the reins and pommel, her jacket slid up and her waist was slender and warm in the circle of his hands.

Her smile was mischievous as he climbed up on his own mount.

"What?"

"I just wanted you to know, that kiss wasn't a thanks for how wonderfully you took care of me last night."

"Then what was it?"

She turned Snowflake and with a skilled nudge, sent her down the trail at an easy walk. "That," she called back over her shoulder, the only sound in the still morning other than the clopping of the horses' hooves. "That was just a preview. Like coming attractions at the movies."

Any ability to speak that Doug thought he'd regained was washed away. If that was a preview, he couldn't wait for the main feature. But the ranch was a long way off.

He looked back at Lucy and her foal who'd fallen in behind. "How fast can you walk?"

The horse declined to answer, instead settling into a slow shuffle.

15

"So, the lost is found," Mark greeted her cheerfully as Chelsea entered the ranch house kitchen.

"Seems so." It had taken seven hours to walk Lucy back. A long cold ride, but under a broken sky rather than a freezing rain. It was now mid-afternoon and the sky was once again darkening beneath an overcast. At least she'd be cozy and safe for the next storm.

"Tessa's down for her nap, so you can just relax. Where's Doug?"

"He's out at the isolation barn. He wants to keep the three horses and foal away from the herd until he's sure that they're not contagious."

"Good man."

"The best." Chelsea knew she'd never met a better one.

Mark looked at her curiously, and then headed for the door. "I'll just go and check on him."

"Do you know *anything* about horses?" She didn't know where the tease had come from. Women didn't tease men like Mark Henderson. But Doug had told her how Mark loved to fish, and almost always used an ATV rather than a horse to get there, so she couldn't resist.

He just winked at her and was gone.

Chelsea took a quiet minute to heat some leftover beef vegetable soup before sitting with it at the big kitchen table. It could seat a dozen without crowding. The kitchen was on the border between a generous farm kitchen and a small commercial one. It was cozy but also designed to feed a hungry hoard. She could imagine dinner parties here filled with laughter and good food.

"What would it be like to live here?" she asked the quiet kitchen. "How happy would it be?"

"Quite happy."

Chelsea startled and almost lost her soupspoon to the floor. For a startled second she thought the kitchen had answered her.

Then she spotted Emily Beale sitting quietly in a deep chair by the kitchen fireplace, a book in her lap. She rose smoothly and came to sit just around the corner of the table from Chelsea.

"The first time I came here, I was in absolute terror."

"You, in terror. Like I believe that."

Emily's smile was always a surprise and it was this time as well. "Seriously. I was engaged to my co-commander of an elite U.S. Army helicopter team—seriously bad from a regulation point of view—and about to meet his parents, one of whom had served twenty years as a Navy SEAL. I'd never gone fishing, never seen a horse up close, and never been to Montana."

Chelsea toyed with her soup. "This place is so amazing though; that must have helped."

"It did. Though not as much as realizing that Mark knew as little about horses as I did." Now Emily's smile turned rather wicked. "Mac and Ama bought the ranch after Mark had gone to West Point."

"So?" Chelsea tried to picture Mark not perfect at something and wasn't coming up with a good image.

"Let's just say that he ended up head over heels in the river and I didn't."

Chelsea held up a hand in salute, but was shocked when Emily actually high-fived it. "Women rule," Chelsea added weakly.

"We do," Emily agreed and offered her a smile of companionship that felt as crazy as everything else that had happened in the last two days.

"I've been very happy here," Emily continued though more as if she was speaking to herself. "It's a good place, as good as any I've ever been."

"I'll miss the ranch when we go."

Emily nodded, but was studying Chelsea carefully.

"What?"

Emily shook her head.

"Nope." Chelsea grabbed onto her bravery. "You don't get to do that."

"Do what?" Emily pretended all innocence.

Chelsea aimed her soupspoon at Emily, "Have that clear a thought and then not share it."

Emily considered for a long moment and then nodded at how that might be a reasonable demand. "Just remember."

"What?"

"You asked."

Chelsea swallowed hard. Why didn't she think she was going to like what came next? She nodded for Emily to go ahead anyway.

"It isn't the ranch that you'll be missing."

Her soupspoon slipped from nerveless fingers and landed in her bowl with a splash.

"Thought so," Emily remarked drily.

"Couldn't you at least have made it a question?"

Emily shook her head. "Why would I, when it isn't one."

"But we haven't even—"

"Doesn't matter. When it's the right one, the particulars don't matter. Trust me, I know."

"The right what? But—" Chelsea managed weakly wondering why she was trying to argue. She'd never met a man like Doug Daniels, a man who simply shone with the love inside him. He had such a passion for the land and the horses.

During the long, cold ride back from the fishing cabin, she and Doug had warmed the time with stories. He'd told her about his experiences overseas, so different from her own tramp abroad. In all of her travels, she'd never found anyone so easy to be with.

And the way he'd knelt before her in the cabin, naked and beautiful and so worried about offending as he treated her abraded legs with stinky liniment.

The way he'd held her last night. There couldn't be another man anywhere who wouldn't have taken advantage of the situation. But not Doug with his soldier's honor.

"I—"

But Emily was no longer there to explain things to. In the big kitchen was only the warm crackling of the fire, Chelsea, and a bowl of soup.

16

Doug was slumped on his couch. The grumbling in his stomach complained about missing dinner up at the main house; too frustrated to whip up something in his own kitchen. He hadn't been able to go because of what else he'd find there. What he was wanting so badly.

The knock on his front door had him racing to answer it. "Is Lucy…o…kay?" The only knock he'd been expecting had been Logan's if Lucy had a relapse. His nervous system was not ready for the vivid redhead standing on his front porch.

"Hi!" Her smile was big and again mischievous.

He had the feeling that he was suddenly in deep trouble.

"Do I get invited in? If not, I'm taking Emily's special homemade pizza back with me. She said that it's one of your favorites."

That's when he focused on the large covered tray Chelsea was carrying. Emily was an amazing cook, had won the hearts of Mac, himself, and every one of the ranch hands with a beef stew on her first visit to the ranch. But it was her from-scratch pizza that blew Doug away.

"Uh—" He looked back up at Chelsea. "I'd like to invite you in, but I don't think that's the best idea. Because if I do—"
If he did, he couldn't be accountable for keeping his hands off her a second time. Last night he'd liked the brave and competent woman, and lusted after the redheaded knockout. On the long ride back, he'd also come to admire her deeply. She'd made some hard choices on her path, who hadn't. But hers had always come straight from the heart.

"—If you do invite me in," Chelsea picked up for him as she eased him slowly backward with the leading edge of a tray of pizza, "we just might enjoy ourselves beyond all imagining."

"Something like that," he managed.

"Good. I'm counting on it." She kicked off her boots, and carried the tray through his living room and into the kitchen as if she'd always lived here. "You were raised in a barn. Close the door; it's cold out there."

Helpless to argue, he did as she suggested and followed her into the kitchen.

"I'm sorry," she set the tray on top of the cold stove.

"Sorry for what?"

"The pizza and the tiny ranch house tour are going to have to come later. I can't wait any longer." She shed her gloves and jacket and dropped them to the floor. Then she walked straight into his arms.

17

They had cold pizza while sitting among their clothes on the kitchen floor. Doug reheated some after they'd made prolonged use of the living room sofa; long enough to have to restock the fire. They finished the last of the meal on their way upstairs when she went hunting for the bedroom; a search that was gloriously rewarded.

"Did we miss anywhere?" Chelsea lay sprawled over him, sore in so many wonderful ways. She'd never done anything like this. Never had so much fun having sex either. Doug's blend of powerful yet gentle, of roughly needy and deeply giving had enthralled and sated her like no one before.

"Uh, big bathroom, second bedroom, home office."

"Oh." They'd probably kill each other if they tried for all of them tonight.

"Back porch lit by June moonlight," he mumbled on. "There's a set of waterfalls with a hot spring about a three-hour hike above the fishing cabin that shouldn't scare off a woman who had hiked in the Himalayas. The open prairie on a warm May afternoon where you'd outshine the sun. I'll show you—"

She put her fingers over his mouth to stop him and he kissed the fingertips.

"I like your imagination," she propped herself up on his chest and looked down into his dark eyes. "So the sex is good."

"Incredible," he agreed.

"You love what you do?"

"I do," he agreed just as equably.

"And you've spent two days and two nights fantasizing about having me beside you forever."

"Yep."

She waited for it. Perhaps it was unfair. Giving a man his favorite food then making love to him multiple times; his defenses were pretty much gone.

But there was no shock of recognition at what she'd just said. No startled disclaimer that he wasn't dumb enough to extrapolate two days into a lifetime.

"Whoa there!" It was supposed to have been a tease.

"As the lady once said," he grinned up at her. "Hello! Not a horse."

"Hold on."

"The way I figure it," she could feel his chest rippling against hers as he spoke, "it's actually been two days and three nights. I think we're closer to sunrise than sunset. So, we've already made it twenty-five percent longer than what you said."

"Douglas," she warned him.

"Just Doug. Nobody calls me Douglas, not even Mom."

"Douglas!"

"Yes, Chelsea?"

"Does it make any sense?"

"Nope. Not a bit," and his voice remained merry.

"Aren't you even a little surprised?"

"Nope."

"Why not?" Chelsea's own thoughts were in such turmoil, they might as well be a wheeling herd of horses.

"Got over it in the barn while taking care of Lucy."

"A *horse* told you that we'd be spending our lives together? Even from Horseboy, I'm not buying that one." *Spending our lives together* and still no flinch on his part. She checked in with herself. Even stranger, there wasn't a flinch on her part either.

"No, from Mark."

"Mark?" was all she managed.

"Yep! I was out making sure Lucy and the other horses were all settled in, when he came out to the barn."

"What did he say?" Chelsea was pretty sure she didn't want to know. She went to roll off Doug's chest, but he trapped her in place with a hand resting lightly on her hip. Just enough to tell her she was retreating, not enough that she couldn't get away. *Fine!*

She could take it if he could, and rolled back into place.

"He said that you were one of the nicest young women he'd ever met and I'd never find any better. That part I agreed with readily enough," Doug nodded emphatically as if marking such an outrageous statement as simple truth. "And if I was too stupid to see that you were already in love with me, he'd be glad to pound some sense into me."

She let his "love" statement go by for the moment.

"Do you think they set us up?" She wasn't sure if she'd be angry or not, but wanted to know.

"My question too. Mark said no. Emily's not much sneakier than he is, so I'm guessing the answer there is also no. I suspect that we did this to ourselves."

"We…what?" But it was lame and she knew it. Emily had said the same thing, or why else was Chelsea here in bed with Doug?

This time when she pushed away, he let her go.

Chelsea wrapped a blanket around her shoulders and moved to look out the window. The yard rolled away into the darkness. Faint lights marked the barns, a lone porch light up at the main ranch house.

Could she be happy here? Working horses, sharing this gorgeous land with visitors? In a heartbeat.

With this man?

Doug slipped up behind her and wrapped his arms across her shoulders.

How was she supposed to know something like that so quickly?

Even if she already did?

Emily had said she recognized that he was the right one for her. As if she knew what love looked like. Well, if any woman did, it would be Emily Beale.

Chelsea leaned back against Doug—and the rightness was there. It ran so deep that she couldn't imagine being anywhere else.

"I was thinking," he whispered in her ear.

She hummed with pleasure, couldn't help herself.

"How about we just try each other on for size? You and me."

"And the horses."

She could more feel his laugh than hear it.

"And the horses. We'll agree to make no decisions at all until the snow melts."

"But there isn't any snow," she waved a hand toward the window.

He didn't speak, instead he pointed. In the faint lights, she could see the first flakes spinning down out of the sky.

"A white Christmas," she managed on a tight breath.

He wrapped his arms around her a little more tightly.

Doug was right, they needed time to decide if what was between them was real or not.

But she knew. Her wandering days were done.

A white Christmas together.

Chelsea turned in Doug's arms and kissed him. She knew right down to her heart that this was only the first of so many to come.

About the Author

M. L. Buchman has over 40 novels in print. His military romantic suspense books have been named Barnes & Noble and NPR "Top 5 of the Year," nominated for the Reviewer's Choice Award for "Top 10 Romantic Suspense of 2014" by RT Book Reviews, and twice Booklist "Top 10 of the Year" placing two of his titles on their "The 101 Best Romance Novels of the Last 10 Years." In addition to romance, he also writes thrillers, fantasy, and science fiction.

In among his career as a corporate project manager he has: rebuilt and single-handed a fifty-foot sailboat, both flown and jumped out of airplanes, designed and built two houses, and bicycled solo around the world.

He is now making his living as a full-time writer on the Oregon Coast with his beloved wife. He is constantly amazed at what you can do with a degree in Geophysics. You may keep up with his writing by subscribing to his newsletter at: www.mlbuchman.com.

Christmas at Steel Beach

-a Night Stalkers romance-
(excerpt)

U.S. Navy Chief Steward Gail Miller held on for dear life as the small boat raced across the warm seas off West Africa.

The six Marines driving the high-speed small unit riverine boat appeared to think that scaring the daylights out of her was a good sport. It was like a Zodiac rubber dinghy's big brother. It was a dozen meters long with large machine guns mounted fore and aft. The massive twin diesels sent it jumping off every wave, even though the rollers in the Gulf of Guinea were less than a meter high today.

Gail wondered if they were making the ride extra rough just for her or were they always like this; she suspected the latter. Still she wanted to shout at them like Bones from *Star Trek*: *I'm a chef, not a soldier, dammit.* But being a good girl from South Carolina, she instead kept her mouth shut and stared at her fast-approaching new billet.

The USS *Peleliu* was an LHA, a Landing Helicopter Assault ship. She could deliver an entire Marine Expeditionary Unit with her helicopters and amphibious craft. Twenty-five hundred Navy and Marines personnel aboard and it would be her job to feed them. All the nerves she'd been feeling for the last five days about her new posting had finally subsided, buried beneath the tidal wave of wondering if she was going to survive to even reach the *Peleliu.*

At first, the ship started out as black blot on the ocean, silhouetted by the setting sun that was turning the sky from a golden orange over to more of a dark rose color.

Then the ship got bigger.

And bigger.

In a dozen years in the Navy she'd been aboard an aircraft carrier only once, and it lay twenty minutes behind her. She'd been there less than a half hour from when the E-2 Hawkeye had trapped on the deck. They'd shipped her to the *Peleliu* so fast she wanted to check herself and see if she was radioactive.

It didn't matter though; she was almost there. From down in the little riverine speed boat, her new ship looked huge. The second largest ships in the whole Navy, after the aircraft carriers, were the helicopter carriers.

Gail knew that the *Peleliu* was the last of her class, all of her sister ships already replaced by newer and better vessels, but even six months or a year aboard before her decommissioning would be a fantastic opportunity for a Chief Steward. Maybe that's why they'd assigned Gail to this ship, someone to fill in before the decommissioning.

Fine with her.

She was still unsure how she'd actually landed the assignment. She'd spent a half-dozen years working on the Perry Class frigates as a CS, a culinary specialist. Her first Chief Steward billet had been at SUBASE Bangor in Washington state feeding submariners while ashore until she thought she'd go mad. She missed the ship's galleys and the life aboard.

Then she'd applied for a transfer, never in her life expecting to land Chief Steward on an LHA. After the aircraft carriers, they were the premier of Navy messes. Chefs vied for years to get these slots and she'd somehow walked into this one.

No, girl! You've cooked Navy food like a demon for over a decade to earn this posting. Her brain's strong insistence that she'd earned this did little to convince her.

And she hadn't walked into this, she'd flown. It had taken three days: Seattle, New York, London, Madrid, and Dakar, each with at least six hours on the ground, but never enough to get a room and sleep. And then an eyeblink on the aircraft carrier.

It didn't matter. It was hers now for whatever reason and she couldn't wait.

The LHA really did look like an aircraft carrier. She knew it was shorter and narrower, but from down here on the waves, it loomed and towered. *One heck of an impressive place to land, girl.* She could feel the "new posting" nerves fighting back against the "near death" nerves of her method of transit over the waves.

The flattop upper deck didn't overhang as much as an aircraft carrier, but that was the only obvious difference. Like a carrier, the Flight Deck was ruled over by a multi-story communications tower superstructure and its gaggle of antennas above.

On the deck she could see at least a half-dozen helicopters and people working on them, probably putting them away for the end of the day. It seemed odd to Gail that they were operating so far from the carrier group. It had taken an hour even at the riverine's high speed to reach the *Peleliu* and she appeared to be out here alone; not another ship in sight.

In the fading sunset, the ship's lights were showing more and more as long rows of bright pinpricks. The flattop was at least five stories above the water.

The riverine boat circled past the bow and rocketed toward the stern. Gail had departed the aircraft carrier down a ladder on the outside of the hull amidships. But here they approached the stern.

That was the big difference with the LHAs; they had a massive Well Deck right inside the rear of the ship. She'd seen pictures, but when her orders came, they'd been for "Immediate departure." No time to read up on the *Peleliu.* So, she'd learn on the job.

A massive stern ramp was being lowered down even as they circled the boat. It was as if the entire cliff-like stern of the boat was opening like a giant mailbox, the door hinging down to make a steel beach in the water.

Also like a mailbox, it revealed a massive cavern inside. Fifteen meters wide, nearly as tall, and a football field deep; it penetrated into the ship at sea level. Landing craft could be driven right inside the ship's belly, loaded with vehicles from the internal garages or Marines from the barracks, and then floated back out.

The last of the fast equatorial sunset was fading from the sky as the riverine whipped around the stern at full-speed in a turn she was half sure would toss her overboard into the darkness, and roared up to the steel beach.

Inside the cavern of the Well Deck, dim red lights suggested shapes and activities she couldn't quite make out.

# # #

The sunset was still flooding the Well Deck through the gap above the *Peleliu's* unopened stern ramp as U.S. Navy Chief Petty Officer Sly Stowell did his best to look calm. After nineteen years in, it was his job to radiate steadiness to his customers, the troops he was transporting. That wasn't a problem.

He was also supposed to actually *be* calm during mission preparations, but it never seemed to work that way. A thousand hours of drill still never prepared him for the adrenaline rush of a live op and tonight he'd been given the "go for operation." This section of the attack—presently loading up on his LCAC hovercraft deep inside the belly of the USS *Peleliu*—was all his.

"Get a Navy move-on, boys," he shouted to the Ranger platoon loading up, "'nuff of this lazy-ass Army lollygag."

A couple of the newbies flinched, but all the old hands just grinned at him and kept pluggin' along. They all wore camo gear and armored vests. Their packs were only large for this mission, not massive. It was supposed to be an in and out, but it was always better to be prepared.

Two of the old hands wore Santa hats, had their Kevlar brain buckets with the clipped on night-vision gear dangling off their rifles. It was December first and he liked the spirit of it, celebrating the season, though he managed not to smile at them. It was the sworn duty of every soldier to look down on every other, especially for the Navy to look down on everyone else. It was only what the ground pounders and sky jockeys deserved, after all.

The *Peleliu* was a Navy ship, even if she'd switched over from carrying Marines to now having a load of Army aboard. The transition had worried him at first. Two decades of Marines and their ways had been uprooted six months ago and now a mere platoon of U.S. Army 75th Rangers had taken their place. The swagger was much the same though.

But *Peleliu* had also taken on a company from the Army's Special Operations Aviation Regiment—their secret helicopter corps. They didn't swagger, they flew. And, as much as Sly might feel disloyal to his branch of the Service, they tended to bring much more interesting operations than the Marines.

He could hear the low roar as the engines on the Ranger vehicles selected for this mission were started up in the *Peleliu's* garage decks. The three vehicles rolled down the ramp toward Sly's hovercraft moments later.

Normally it would have taken an hour of shuffling vehicles to extricate the ones they wanted from their tight parking spaces. But fifty Rangers needed far fewer vehicles than seventeen hundred Marines. The whole ship now had an excess of space. Having a tenth of the military personnel aboard had meant that two-thirds of the Navy personnel had also moved on to other billets.

Sly had been thrilled when his application to stay had been granted. It might not be the best career move, but the *Peleliu* was his and he wanted to ride her until the day she died.

It had also turned out to be a far more interesting choice, though he hadn't known it at the time. Marines were all about *invade that country*, or *provide disaster relief for that flood or earthquake.* The 160th SOAR and the U.S. Rangers were about fast and quiet ops that only rarely were released to the news.

He watched as his crew began guiding the M-ATVs onto his hovercraft. They looked like Humvees on steroids. They were taller, had v-shaped hulls for resistance against road mines, and looked far meaner.

He'd been assigned to the LCAC hovercraft since his first day aboard. First as mechanic, then loadmaster, navigator, and finally pilot. And he'd never gotten over how much she looked like a hundred-ton shoebox without the lid.

He kept an eye on Nika and Jerome as they guided the first M-ATV down the internal ramp of the *Peleliu* and up the front-gate ramp of the LCAC. He trusted them completely, but he was the craftmaster and it was ultimately his job to make sure it was right.

The "shoebox" presently had her two narrow ends folded down. The tall sides were made up of the four Vericor engines, fans, blowers, defensive armor, and the control and gunnery positions. The front end was folded down revealing the three-lane wide parking area of the LCAC's deck. Between the two massive rear fans to the stern—which still reminded him of the fanboats from his family's one trip down to the Florida Everglades where they had *not* seen an alligator—a one-lane wide rear ramp was folded down toward the stern.

The LCAC was the size of a basketball court, though her sides towered twice as high as the basket. She filled the wood-planked Well Deck from side to side and could carry an Abrams M1A1 Main Battle Tank from here right up onto the beach. Those days were gone, though. Now it was the noise of Army Rangers and their M-ATVs filling the cavernous space in which even a sneeze echoed painfully.

Still, the old girl could handle them and it had instilled a new life in the ship. She'd been Sly's home for the entire two decades of his Naval career and he didn't look forward to giving her up. He sometimes felt as if they both were hanging on out of sheer stubbornness. Hell of a thought for a guy still in his thirties. Hanging on by his fingernails? Sad.

He'd considered getting a life. Mustering out, having a pension in place and starting a new career. But he loved this one.

And he'd been aboard the eight-hundred foot ship long enough that she was now called a two-hundred and fifty meter ship instead. This was his home.

Eighteen year-old Seaman Stowell had nearly shit his uniform the day he'd reported aboard. She'd been patrolling off Mogadishu, Somalia then. In the two decades since, they'd circled the globe in both directions, though since the arrival of SOAR most of their operations had been around Africa. In nineteen years he'd traded East Africa for West Africa… and a lifetime between.

As he did before every mission, he willed this mission to please go better than the disastrous Operation Gothic Serpent—the failure immortalized by the movie *Black Hawk Down* that had unfolded ashore within days of his arrival aboard.

Sly didn't feel all that different, except he no longer wanted to shit his pants before battle. He still had to consciously calm down though.

Instead of a humdrum routine settling in after the Marines Expeditionary Unit's departure, the Rangers and SOAR had amped it back up.

SOAR was a kick-ass team, even by Navy standards. That they also had the number one Delta Force operator on the planet permanently embedded with them only meant that Sly's life was never dull.

That was one of the reasons that Sly was looking forward to this operation. When Colonel Michael Gibson was involved, you knew it was going to be a hell-raiser.

They had the first M-ATV in place and locked down. The second one rolled up the ramp. Lieutenant Barstowe, the Rangers' commander, came up beside him with his Santa hat still in place.

"Chief."

"Lieutenant."

"That's one battle-rigged and two ambulance M-ATVs. Why don't I like that ratio?"

"Because you're a smart man, Chief Stowell." The lieutenant moved up the ramp to talk with the driver of the third vehicle still waiting its turn.

They were definitely going into it heavy. That's what finally calmed Sly's nerves. It was the preparation he hated, once on the move he no longer had spare time to worry that he'd forgotten something. And they were definitely going in ready for the worst.

At least he wasn't the only one sweating it. Today was pretty typical December off the West African coast, ninety degrees and ninety percent humidity. Even the seawater from the Gulf of Guinea was limp with tepid heat as it sloshed against the outside of the hull with a flat slap and echo inside that resounded inside the Well Deck.

The last of the vehicles rolled up onto the LCAC hovercraft. For the Landing Craft, Air Cushion hovercraft—technically pronounced L.C.A.C. but more commonly El-Cack! like you were about to throw up—forty tons of vehicles and fifty Rangers was about a half load. But still he was going to keep an eagle eye on them. These young bucks might think they were the bad-asses, but until they'd faced down a Naval Chief Petty Officer—well, that was never going to happen as long as he was in the Navy.

Nika and Jerome guided the last of the vehicles into position at the center of gravity. Nika had been on his boat for two tours now and she'd better re-up next month because he had no idea who he'd ever find to replace her. She worked quickly on chaining down the third vehicle and then gave him a thumbs up. Jerome had six months as his mechanic, but had the routine down and echoed Nika's signal. His engineer and his navigator reported ready.

The crew had already preflighted the craft, but he liked to do a final walk-around himself. There was only a foot between either side of the LCAC and the Well Deck walls.

The wooden decking along the bottom of the Well Deck was just clear of the wash of the ocean waves, so he didn't need waders to do the inspection. For conventional landing craft that needed water to move around in, they could ballast down the stern, which lowered the ship to flood the Well Deck a meter deep or more. However, his hovercraft didn't need such concessions. It was better this way. They could lift off dry without shedding a world of salt spray in all directions.

"Nika," he called as he headed down to start his inspection, "get that stern gate open." During the loading, the last of the sunset had disappeared, near darkness filled in the gap above the big door.

The Well Deck's lights flickered as they were switched over from white to red for nighttime operations. They hadn't flickered when he first came aboard, but she was feeling her age. He patted the inside of the *Peleliu's* hull in sympathy as he reached the wooden planking that supported his LCAC. The huge rear gate let out a groan and began tipping out and down toward the sea.

His hovercraft was ninety feet long and fifty wide and there actually wasn't much to see during his inspection, which was a good thing. The deflated skirts that would trap the air from the four gas turbine engines, delivering over twenty-thousand horsepower of lift and driving force, now hung in limp folds of thick black rubber. Patches covering tears and bullet holes from prior missions dotted the rippling surface. Above the rubber skirt, the aluminum sides were battered from the hard use—partly bad-guy assholes with rifles and partly harsh weather operations.

Sly saw the former as badges of courage for the old craft…and did his best not to recall how the latter was earned when nasty cross seas had slammed his craft into the sides of the Well Deck entrance. He was a damn good pilot, but there were limits to what a man could do when the ship went one way, the seas another, and his hovercraft a third.

He was halfway around his craft when he first heard it, the high whine of an incoming boat. It hadn't been there a moment before. The Well Deck acted like a giant acoustical horn, gathering all sounds from dead astern and amplifying and focusing them like a gunshot at anyone inside the cavernous Well Deck at the time. Often you'd hear a boat before you saw it, especially at night.

He stood at the foot of the rear ramp of the hovercraft and turned, but there were no lights to see.

Then there were, incredibly close aboard. A small unit riverine craft by the arrangement of the blinding white lights that had him raising an arm to save his eyes.

The riverine was carving a high speed turn as if they intended to run right up the stern gate and into the Well Deck.

They cut their speed at the last moment with a hard reverse of the engines, but he knew it was too late for him.

The bow wave rushed up the Well Deck planking ahead of the riverine, driven bigger and faster by the abrupt nose-down of the decelerating craft. The wave came high enough to soak him to mid-calf and made him sit down abruptly. The wave washed part way up the rear ramp of his hovercraft before receding—totally soaking his butt.

He wondered who he could blame for this one.

In a moment, he was going to stand up and the fifty Rangers standing on the LCAC's loading deck were going to be laughing their asses off at the Navy's expense.

That just wasn't right. Sly glared over at the small riverine craft, squinting against the bright array of lights so that he could see who to blame. The bow section folded forward and allowed a tall woman wearing a duffle over one shoulder and carrying a small black case to dismount. Then the craft began backing away from the Well Deck even as the bow section was pulled back up. He didn't get a good look at any of them. *The dogs!*

The woman walked up close to Sly and stopped to look down at him.

That initial impression of tall was combined with Navy fit, and a uniform that showed it off in the best way. Her short tousle of dark red hair hung perfectly as if she'd just brushed it rather than gone for a ride on a craft that could hit thirty-five knots. She wore an emblem of a large crescent-shaped "C" over four horizontal stripes. The "C" marked her as a Steward, the four stripes as the new Chief Steward they'd been told to expect.

She looked like a breath of fresh air.

Truth be told, she looked like the goddamn goddess Venus rising from the water as she stepped out onto the last retreating sheen of seawater that was washing back off the deck under her boots.

He stood to greet her properly.

A roll of laughter sounded behind him and Sly turned—remembering a moment too late as he turned his back on the new Chief—the butt of his uniform was still sopping wet.

∗∗∗

Available at fine retailers everywhere
More information at:
www.mlbuchman.com

Other works by M.L. Buchman

Where Dreams Reside
Maria's Christmas Table
Where Dreams Unfold
Where Dreams Are Written

Dieties Anonymous
Cookbook from Hell: Reheated
Saviors 101

Thrillers
Swap Out!
One Chef!
Two Chef!

SF/F Titles
Nara
Monk's Maze

Made in the USA
San Bernardino, CA
21 November 2016